For Claire
L. U.

For my mom, who does it herself
M. V.

Text copyright © 2015 by Linda Urban
Illustrations copyright © 2015 by Madeline Valentine

First edition 2015

Library of Congress Catalog Card Number 2014939355
ISBN 978-0-7636-6176-2

15 16 17 18 19 20 CCP 10 9 8 7 6 5 4 3 2 1

Printed in Shenzhen, Guangdong, China

This book was typeset in Berkeley.
The illustrations in this book are graphite drawings
printed on watercolor paper and painted in gouache.

Candlewick Press
99 Dover Street
Somerville, Massachusetts 02144

visit us at www.candlewick.com

Little Red Henry

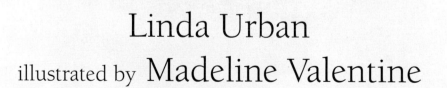

Linda Urban

illustrated by Madeline Valentine

CANDLEWICK PRESS

Ever since time began,

Mama and Papa and Mem and Sven had loved and cuddled
and smooched and squeezed their little redheaded Henry.
They had made his breakfast and picked out his clothes and
ferried him here and there, and if he hadn't gotten so big,
he might never have known the feeling of the
earth under his feet, they had carried him about so.

Frankly, little redheaded Henry was sick of it.

"I'm not a baby," said Henry.

"Of course you're not," said Mama. "Now, sit down in your itty-bitty chair
and let Mommy make you breakfast."

The rest of the family was not to be outdone.

"Let me," said Papa.

"Let me," said Mem.

"Let me," said Sven.

"No, thank you," said Henry. "I can do it myself."

And he did.

After breakfast, Mama swooped in low. "Let Mommy brush your widdle toofers." The rest of the family raced to the bathroom, elbowing and calling dibs.

"Let me!" cried Papa.

"Let me!" shouted Mem.

"Let me!" hollered Sven.

"No, thank you," said Henry.

"Pretty please?" whimpered Papa.

"Just the molars?"

"I can do it myself," said Henry.

And he did.

It seemed like a good time to visit his friend Gibson.
Henry went to his bedroom to get dressed. As usual,
his clothes had been laid out for the day.
"I'd prefer something else," said Henry.

"Something sporty," said Papa.

"Something snuggly," said Mem.

"Something snazzy," said Sven.

"I can choose them myself," said Henry.

And he did.

Henry headed next door to his friend Gibson's house.
"Let me call Gibson's granny and make arrangements," cried Mama.

"Let me," said Papa.

"Let me," said Mem.

"Let me," said Sven.

But Henry was already knocking—
with his own bare knuckles—
on Gibson's front door.

"I can do it myself," he said.

And he did.

All day, Henry and Gibson played in Gibson's backyard.

They pushed each other on the swing and crafted
castles in the sandbox and commanded robot armies.

They teeter-totted and monkey-barred
and triumphed gloriously on the battlefield.

It was amazing.

At supper, Henry poured his own glass of milk

without

spilling

a drop.

He cut his own lasagna and buttered his own bread
and proudly devoured every detestable pea on his plate.

The rest of the family had no appetite.

They were listless. Adrift. Without Henry
to do things for, they had no purpose.
"What are we to do?" they asked one another.

"What do you *want* to do?" asked Henry.

"Well . . ." said Mama.

"There might . . ." said Papa.

"Be *something*. . . ." said Mem and Sven.

All evening long, Mama, Papa, Mem, Sven, and Henry practiced and painted and tapped and typed.

They waltzed and wallpapered and scribbled and scratched.

It grew very, very late. Henry went upstairs.
He put on his pajamas all by himself.

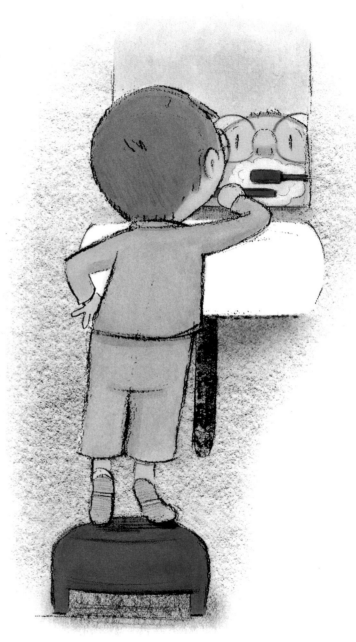

He brushed his teeth all by himself.
He climbed into his bed all by himself.

He was all by himself.

"Could somebody please tuck me in?"

"Oh!" said Mama. "Of course!"

"Let me," said Papa.

"Let me," said Mem.

"Let me," said Sven.

"You can all tuck me in," said Henry. "Tonight, anyway."

Mama and Papa and Mem and Sven loved and cuddled
and snuggled and squeezed their little redheaded Henry.
They fluffed up his pillows and tucked in his covers and
wished him sweet dreams and sang him a long lullaby . . .

most of which he did not hear through his own soft snores.